Musings

(A Collection of 8 Short Stories and a Novella)

Musings

(A Collection of 8 Short Stories and a Novella)

Manjari Narayana

PARTRIDGE

A Penguin Random House Company

To order additional copies of this book, contact
Partridge India
000 800 10062 62
orders.india@partridgepublishing.com

www.partridgepublishing.com/india

CONTENTS

FOR MY BUNDLE OF JOY HIYA

FOR MY GRAND PARENTS

THANK YOU NOTE

First of all, a special word of gratitude to my reverential parents for their whole-hearted encouragement and support. Secondly, I would like to thank my sister Nupur and my kid sister Tanushree for providing inputs that have proved handy in my workmanship. You are my real heroes!!

To Mritunjay ji, my husband who is the leading light of my life as also to daughter Hiya and niece Swastika who have been an invaluable inspiration for the book.

Jaya ji and my mentor Abdul sir for your guidance and suggestions and for instilling hope in me in the most trying times.

A sincere word of thanks to *bhaiya* O.P. Rai *ji* and Dr. Nirmal Chopra for all the inspiration and positive words. It has been a privilege to have you as a buddy and well-wisher.

Thanks to Chaman uncle and Mrs Canteenwala, for being a teacher-cum-friend, philosopher and guide. Wish you a very long life!

My *whatsapp* friends, for their unending jokes and exuberance. It is because of you that my journey as a writer has been smooth sailing.

Finally, a special word of acknowledgement to Mr. A Kumar and S. Agarwal without whose help this book would have been a dream unfulfilled.

SHORT STORIES

HEAD OR TAIL - 1

A arti fulfilled all the essential pre-requisites of a perfect homemaker offering nonchalant compliance to the wishes of her sadist and nagging spouse Rajan, no matter how petty so-much-so that her restraint and self-possession was talked about amongst relatives, friends and in the immediate neighbourhood. Her sons Rachit and Sanchit though, smothered by their father's affection, were invariably papa's boys.

It were the wee hours of Monday morning and Aarti had just finished with packing the school tiffins for her sons. Numerous chores were still lined-up and she took care to expedite each one with due caution. Sometimes even the most efficient of servants found it hard to match-up with her outstanding pace.

'Aarti, why is my breakfast not ready yet? I have to leave for an urgent meeting....' Rajan hollered in his usual style.

'The meal is done!' said Aarti as she served Rajan's favourite piping-hot potato curry with crisp *parathas*. Rajan had been very fussy when it came to food and would not have relished it otherwise.

After Rajan had left, Aarti finished with all the household chores and sat in front of the T.V. to catch-up with her favourite show. During the ad-break, she drew out her shopping list from the chest of drawers to peek-a-look at the list of things she had to buy. 'Lo! I have exchanged my shopping list with Rajan's important official papers and Rajan will not be back for lunch today or else I could have rectified my mistake!' Aarti's heart sank as she thought about the ramifications of her misdemeanour.

Aarti, without a moments delay, informed Bindiya, her immediate neighbour and bosom friend about the day's incident and why she had decided to call-off their shopping plans. Bindiya was a fashionable lady and a social butterfly and whenever Rajan would not turn up for lunch or was on an official tour to a different city, the ladies would gang-up and have a ball!

Quite contrary to Aarti's expectations, Rajan returned home in the evening looking jubilant than ever. Apparently, the arrival of his uncle just in the nick of time had saved the day. Rajan and his uncle shared some light moments over cups of tea and light snacks prepared by Aarti. The next morning Rajan's uncle presented a georgette sari in shades of orange and purple to his *bahurani* and took leave.

In the days to come, an unusual spring in Rajan's step told a different story. Strands of auburn hair enmeshed between his shirt buttons and lipstick stains on his pocket kerchief made Aarti smell a rat!

'I shall not rest till I have found out the truth!' Aarti thought as she lay in bed tossing and turning. The happenings of the day had rendered her wakeful and restless.

The next day when Rajan left for office, Aarti pursued him in an auto-rickshaw unbeknown. On reaching the office premises, Aarti waited near the hallway entrance trying to peek-a-look at the comings and goings. She witnessed a tall, lanky woman accompany Rajan inside his office chamber. When the hallway was practically deserted, she peered through the keyhole of Rajan's chamber and was stupefied to witness the two in a compromising situation.

'So he is having a good time with this cock-eyed slut while I slog day in and day out!' Aarti thought as tears rolled down her cheeks almost effortlessly. She quickly retraced her steps homewards and behaved as if nothing had happened.

During the afternoon Aarti narrated the entire incident to Bindiya.

'So things have come to such a passé. 'Why don't you divorce him? What has this 15 years of married-life brought you except tears and woes...?' Bindiya remarked.

'In a way you are right...but...where will that lead me? And after the divorce that slut will be free to marry him. No... no..., I will not divorce my husband and let things move their way,' Aarti stated.

Bindiya tried hard to think of a way out of the ticklish situation. After a few minutes at mulling over the problem at hand she came up with an idea 'May be you can start working. That can help a lot in boosting your self-esteem and at the same time you will find a diversion from these thorny issues.'

'Hmmmm... I will give it a thought,' Aarti commented. The honking of the school-bus horn made Aarti realize that it was time for her sons to be back home after a wearisome day at school. Having made a promise to remain in touch, the friends kissed each other goodbye. The idea of finding a job seemed to have hit-off well with Aarti!

Meanwhile Aarti tried experimenting with a new idea and did not inform even her best friend Bindiya about it. Her plain logic was that any woman inhabiting the planet would have done it to save her marriage from the grisly shadows haunting her conjugal life. In the evening she slipped away to purchase some sexy, branded lingerie with the intention of seducing her husband and waited for the night to dawn to show her steamier side.

When Rajan retired to bed after meals, Aarti tuned-in to some sizzling *bollywood* numbers and began her strip-tease act self-assured that she could deliver better than his new-found love. Rajan who was appalled to witness the scene before him couldn't help but remark 'Is something wrong....? Did you pick a fight with one of our neighbours or have one of our sons offended you with their pranks yet again...? I'm dog tired, let me sleep peacefully,' he said laughing a hearty laugh to witness his wife in a bold new avatar.

While Rajan tried to catch-up on his sleep, Aarti went to an obscure corner of her house where she could cry her heart out. Even the last ditch effort to save the situation had failed and there was simply none in her household to understand the pain that she was going through. 'These men find cheap women a real turn-on. Decent and simple women don't appeal to their tastes,' she mumbled.

Rajan was very much opposed to the idea of his wife pursuing a career. However, with some cajoling, the idea of teaching the primary section in a nearby Christian Missionary School was agreed upon. Aarti joined school and was entrusted with the task of teaching Hindi and Physical Education to third and fourth graders.

HEAD OR TAIL - 2

Teaching young children was an altogether fresh experience and the students simply loved their dimpled Ms. Aarti to the hilt. Aarti proved herself a dedicated and affectionate teacher. She had been especially fond of girls in her class who were less boisterous than their male counterparts.

Amongst the fourth graders she witnessed one particularly quiet child. She was gaunt and Aarti learnt that the girl brought very little tiffin and sometimes went without any food during the recess hours. Her name was Mini. Mini managed decent grades in school her impoverished background notwithstanding.

Aarti began sharing her tiffin with Mini. At first Mini had been hesitant to accept the handouts, however with some persuasion she eventually agreed. Aarti learnt from the conversations that she had with Mini that her father had expired in a car accident and her mother had taken-up sewing and tailoring job to make a living.

Aarti started bringing *pulao* and homemade sweets for Mini. Aarti also helped Mini make friends in school and instilled in her students the spirit of sharing.

With passage of time, Aarti became Mini's close confidante and buddy. One day Mini requested Aarti to visit her home. Aarti could feel words taken out of her mouth. She decided to visit Mini's home the very same day, after school hours.

When the two reached Mini's home premises during the afternoon, Aarti noticed a dilapidated structure with **Sneha's Boutique** mentioned at the entrance.

Upon entering, Aarti saw two rooms adjacent to each other, one of which had been converted into a boutique with modest displays and a small work-area where Sneha (Mini's mother) sat at the sewing-machine completing the heavy backlog. She was coughing incessantly.

'Mamma, look who I have brought home today,' screamed Mini.

Oh, Aarti ma'am!' exclaimed Sneha offering a chair to the visiting guest. 'Mini talks about you a lot.'

Aarti gave a wide grin.

'Mini go and prepare special cardamom tea for Ma'am,' ordered Sneha.

While Mini went to prepare the tea, the ladies sat and chatted: 'My husband was a cloth merchant. After he lost his life in a car accident last year, his brothers took possession of all his fortune and wealth through unfair means leaving us to bite the dust. This little house is the sole property we are left with,' said Sneha.

'Your sewing machine is very dated. I'll order a new one for you that will ease your burden remarkably,' Aarti said as she placed the order for an automatic sewing-machine of the latest model online. 'A concoction drink of ginger and honey is a good antidote to ward-off common cough and cold,' recommended Aarti.

Just then Mini entered the room with two cups of steaming tea. 'The brown cup is Aarti ma'am's and the white one, without cardamom, is for you mamma.'

'Can I take Mini home after school twice or thrice in a week,' pleaded Aarti.

'Sure, why not? She is your child as much as she is mine,' Sneha gave the prompt reply.

From then on Mini became a regular visitor in the Rajan household. She loved the roomy and tastefully furnished interiors as much as she relished the freshly baked cake prepared exclusively for her by Aarti ma'am. She also enjoyed the cartoon series aired on different T.V. channels and played with the toys that Aarti bought for her. Aarti and Mini spent their evenings together at a plush mall or the amusement park.

Whenever Aarti was in a sombre mood, Mini's cardamom tea and the hummable melodies played by her on keyboard, rendered her rejuvenated. 'These hummable and wistful melodies are the only memories I have of papa,' Mini informed.

Aarti had found a daughter in Mini.

As for Rajan he did have reservations on accepting Mini as a new family member but his busy work hours spared him paltry time to crib and complain.

THE INDESTRUCTIBLE MOLE

The walking tracks, situated in the midst of a sprawling campus, boasting of trees in hundreds of varieties and numerous species of birds, had been a paradise for joggers since the bygone days. Frequented by the affluent and opulent classes of the South Delhi area, the sighting of pretty-looking, dapper things at the park was not an uncommon sight.

It was an unusually foggy winter morning. The deciduous trees had shed their leaves and due to thick canopy of fog, the visibility in the park was relatively low. Sighting, cooing and gurgling of birds was a rare occurrence during this time of the year. Nevertheless, the enthusiasm of the fitness-conscious generation was evident from the sighting of an umpteen number of young people at the park striding along, clad from head-to-toe to ward off the chill.

Among the visitors to the jogger's park was a forty-something artist who was occupying one of the benches keenly observing the comings and goings. The people, especially women striding along the walkway were the objects of his interest as they had been the main subjects of his paintings. By now he had painted over four-hundred canvases with women as the central theme.

The painter was observing each passerby minutely paying attention to details such as facial expressions, moods, their anatomy and clothing-styles. However, he was particularly smitten by one lady, who may have been in her early twenties. She was fair, athletic with chiselled-features and looked to be of Punjabi origin. The distinguishable mole on her right cheek set her apart from the rest of the group that she hung-out with. It was evident from the group's conversations that they were, perhaps, fresh MBAs graduates.

The hawk-eyed painter wanted to study the contours of the young lady's face thoroughly before capturing it on canvas. For this he would have to wait for the weather to turn clear.

In about twenty days time the weather had cleared-up and the painter returned with a piece of paper and pencil to prepare a rough sketch of the lady's face which would serve as a reference for his painting. However, all in her group except herself had turned-up. This went on for many days. Every day the artist searched for that face amidst the crowd of passersby but it was nowhere in sight. In the meanwhile he painted her locks, her clothing and the background with utmost care. The painter decided to wait for a few more days for the lady to show-up failing which he would complete the painting from the sheer memories he had of her.

Eventually, the artist painted the contours of the lady's face paying attention to every detail and finishing-off with the mole on the right cheek. He returned to the park the next morning feeling hopeful that he would catch a glimpse of the lady in question. However, she had not turned-up even that day. Eventually his patience gave away and he approached the crowd of youngsters to which the lady had belonged.

'Hello, I am Rajat Khanna, a professional artist. To date I have created thousands of artworks on varied subjects. I caught sight of one of your friends and decided to paint her life-size portrait. I didn't seek her permission though before starting off; sorry for that. Here is my workmanship...But... but...the lady in question is untraceable for quite a few days...' the painter said.

The onlookers were full of awe and admiration at the artistic genius of the man who had created their friend's portrait.

'Our friend, Komal, who has been your musing, has recently been engaged to a Bangalore-based software engineer. Her wedding bells are ringing tomorrow and she has been very busy with the wedding preparations for the last few days,' informed one guy from the group.

'In all likelihood she is expected to be here tomorrow. We will convey to her your message anyway,' said another.

'I hope she comes tomorrow. This painting is a small wedding-gift to her from my side,' informed the artist.

The next day the painter was in his seat at the scheduled hour and waited with bated breath for Komal to turn-up. After a few minutes of wait, Komal's shadow appeared to emerge in the backdrop, her gang of friends following close at her heels. Within a matter of seconds she was standing beside the artist holding the painting in her henna-stained hands. 'This is one of the finest artworks I have ever seen,' she remarked.

The artist's attention had by then drifted to her right cheek. 'Where did that perceptible mole that you once had, disappear?' he questioned inquisitively.

'I had it removed with the help of a plastic surgeon. It was upon the insistence of my wanna-be in-laws,' Komal laughed.

'Oh, then I'll make the necessary corrections in my painting and hand it over to you by evening if you can spare some time,' suggested the artist.

'As I embark on my journey as a daughter-in-law and wife, I shall have to make a lot of adjustments. It will be expected of me to be more responsible and dutiful. The stakes are going to be high. My new family may not shower upon me the unconditional love that I got from my parents. The mole in my portrait is a reminder of my carefree days as a spinster that I spent rolling in the lap of luxury with no "strings attached". My request is you let it remain the way it is,' with these words Komal thanked the painter and ambled homewards leaving others teary-eyed.

PARI'S FANTASY GARDEN

She was tall and upright, though her skin had shown rapid signs of ageing on account of worries, of both financial and emotional nature. She had lost her mother a few years back when the latter had got electrocuted by accident and her incorrigible father very recently on account of liver failure due to excessive drinking habits. Being the sole child to her parents she had no brothers or sisters in whom to repose faith. Her husband, though present, was more or less of an apathetic figure and her three children still quite unsettled.

With her daughter's marriage being finalised recently though, there was some respite for Kanta. She draped her favourite peach sari with ditsy floral prints and applied *bindi* on her callused yet radiant forehead. Collecting her little basket from the shelf, she kissed her kin good bye to catch the train to Delhi.

It was the occasion of Pari's 8th birthday. Kanta had been Pari's nanny when the latter's father Mr Kumar, happened to be posted in Agra a few years ago. Mr. Kumar had of late shifted with his family to Delhi and Kanta had exchanged telephone numbers with Mrs. Kumar as she regarded the couple as her only hope in a soulless and self-absorbed society. She had anticipations that financial help of some sort would be forthcoming from the Kumars during this hour of need. Mrs. Kumar was warmth and affection personified while Mr. Kumar was very illustrious and a respectable name in every household. However, Kanta shared a special bonding with *amma* (Mr. Kumar's mother) and could chatter with her for hours on women-centric subjects.

Kanta's adopted four year old niece Meera had tagged along with her in the train and Kanta had given her the assurance that Pari baby would partake of her discarded toys and clothes some of which Meera could lay her claim on. It did not take very long for the train to reach New Delhi. Holding little Meera's hand, Kanta jostled past the crowd and hailed at an auto-rickshaw that was waiting outside the railway station for to-be customers. The auto-rickshaw squealed to a halt in front of Kanta. '*S-304, Panchsheel Park,*' Kanta said while mounting the vehicle.

This was Kanta's first visit to Delhi and the wide streets teeming with people, the screeching of horns and the greenery along the walkway left her nonplussed. Having been conveyed to her destination safely, Kanta gave the auto-driver his due and stepped inside the Kumar household. Upon entering she witnessed Mr. Kumar in a pensive mood pouring over a book. Towards the right hand side was a garden where Mrs. Kumar was seen engrossed in a diatribe with the event-manager of the birthday party. She apparently seemed vexed at the arrangements not being carried out in the manner as planned. Kanta ambled towards the garden and waited in one corner for the discussion to halt. When Mrs. Kumar seemed somewhat pacified, Kanta intervened - '*Namaste Memsaab.*'

Mrs Kumar turned around to take note of the familiar voice, '*Namaste* Kanta, it is great pleasure to have you here.'

'Where is Pari?' questioned Kanta with hesitation.

'She is in the play area upstairs having a ball with her friends. Ramu *kaka* will escort you there. Be comfortable and enjoy the day.'

It was Pari's birthday and everybody including Kanta could sense the excitement and nervousness in her mother's deportment.

Kanta followed Ramu *kaka* up the flight of steps, with her 4-year-old niece Meera beside all through. The winding wooden staircase led to a hallway which had been converted into a play area for the children to have a rollicking time. Kanta greeted Pari amidst the vociferations who coyly returned some vague reply. Kanta's eyes searched the adjoining rooms for *amma* whom she had not seen in many years. She could witness numerous familiar faces but *amma* was nowhere in sight.

A short while later Mrs. Kumar walked towards the dressing room in consummate haste and beckoned all the female members of the family inside to get ready for the evening gala. Beauticians from a famous salon had been called upon to style their looks.

Kanta went inside one of the rooms and changed her *saree.* She dressed Meera up in an oversized magenta frock. Thereafter the duo curiously ambled into the garden to behold the prettification done for the occasion.

Candy, gingerbread man and fairy props had been erected at regular intervals, the entire area had been bedecked with balloons and streamers, the tables and chairs had been covered with white cloth with pink satin ribbons tied around each one; candy-shaped cut-outs forming into chains cascaded down the window ledges and a large banner carrying Pari's picture with "Pari's Fantasy Garden" pronouncing the party's theme in bold letters set off the entrance.

As the clock struck seven, the congenial and affable hosts ambled towards the garden to welcome arriving guests. Pari looked resplendent in a baby pink gown. The dazzling danglers and the shimmering belt added bling and the boa falling over her shoulders completed the look.

The groovy music set the pace for fun, frolic and games. This was followed by the cake-cutting ceremony and scrumptious meals. The buffet-spread boasted of eight types of salads alone as also wide-ranging cuisine to suit every palate. That evening, Kanta ate like a glutton. By 10.00 p.m. the crowd had dispersed and Mrs. Kumar who had been managing everything was dog-tired. Kanta didn't think it to be an opportune time to un-bosom her worries and decided to take rest.

The following day being a Sunday, proved to be a blessing in disguise for everyone but Mrs. Kumar. She had to manage kitchen chores, entertain guests and *sms* 'thank you' texts to all those who had obliged the family by being present at the function the day before. She started- off with texting messages as she sipped the morning tea. The tea provided some relief to her aching tonsils which had precipitated due to cold weather conditions the day before. Mrs Kumar decided to dispose with the kitchen chores one by one but realised that she could barely handle the pressure.

'Madam I feel you are overworked since the last few days and you need some rest. I'll manage the work.' suggested Ramu *kaka.*

While Mrs Kumar retired to her room to take rest, a string of *sms* beeps ensued in response to her kind-hearted gesture forcing her to keep her cell phone in the silent mode. She checked the thermometer to see if she was running temperature and consulted the family doctor over the phone who prescribed over-the-counter remedies for her condition which was in the incipient stages and advised her complete bed rest.

Behind Ramu *kaka*, Kanta was the first one to learn about *memsaab's* illness. She helped Ramu *kaka* with the kitchen chores while little Meera played with the handcrafted pompoms, the paper rose and savoured the candies that she had received as return gifts at Pari's birthday bash.

As the day progressed, Kanta's hopes of a one-to-one with Mrs Kumar were dashed as the latter lay tightly coiled-up in bed oblivious of the happenings in her immediate vicinity. She quietly handed Pari's present which comprised of a hand-knitted jersey and mittens to Ramu *kaka* and made a last ditch effort to speak with Mr. Kumar's sister: 'Madam my daughter's wedding bells are ringing just after two months in the month of February. Kindly grace the occasion with your presence and bless the young couple for a healthy and enduring conjugal life.'

'We shall definitely attend the wedding and get pictures clicked along with the bride and the groom with the *Taj Mahal* in the backdrop,' quipped Mr Kumar's sister leaving others in the room in splits. In the end Mr Kumar's sister gave Kanta 1100 rupees as token money for the marriage preparations to kick-off in a smooth-sailing manner.

'Thank you madam and *namaste*,' Kanta greeted.

'*Namaste*,' Mr Kumar's sister, her husband and the children chorused.

SHENANIGANS

These days, parents are finding hard to cope-up with their children's endless pranks and wayward ways. Most of these children are almost invariably addicted to junk foods, and trendy gadgets. Gone are the days when children loved playing outdoor games that were invigorating and vivifying. A few will simply shudder at the idea of being woken-up early in the morning and sent packing to school! Keeping late nights and rising late in the day has become an inexorable part of their repertory and reforming such incorrigible souls is turning out to be a back-breaking task for the parents of the current generation.

The seven year old Kilol was no exception to this rule. Though intelligent and quick-witted, her phobia towards studies was a matter of genuine concern for her well-wishers and managing her tantrums a herculean task for her sweet-natured mother, Namrata.

After receiving feedback from several experience ladies, Namrata realised that bringing up a child involved a lot of painstaking efforts and a working knowledge of child psychology was sometimes an added incentive. Namrata was resolved to make an effort in the positive direction even if it required stringent methods, which quite went against her basic nature and had it not been for Kilol's indisposition that day, her 'mission impossible' to remodel Kilol could have well begun!

That day Kilol returned from school with a sore throat and runny nose after having consumed dollops of ice-cream. Namrata, whose love for her daughter knew no bounds naturally had butterflies in her stomach. Without a second's delay she checked the latter's temperature and called the doctor who prescribed a heavy dose of antibiotics and advised complete bed rest. During the period that Kilol was ill, Namrata let her watch her favourite T.V. shows and surf the internet as she felt that imposing restrictions during illness would hinder speedy recovery. At this time, she showered love and affection on Kilol and narrated fables at night-time to infuse wisdom on her impressionable mind.

One thing praiseworthy about Kilol was that her quest for knowledge and inquisitiveness was profound. She would pop-up bizarre queries that would leave Namrata in a tizzy. Namrata had a difficult time finding answers to some of the inexplicable phenomena.

'Mamma, how did the rabbit get over the moon? Mamma, Laakhan says that upon swallowing the orange seed accidently, an orange tree is bound to grow inside my stomach, Laakhan is lying no...?' Kilol would quiz ceaselessly.

It took Kilol nearly a week's time to recover and resume her pranks. Her energy and zest were exemplary for all and sundry.

These days, her mother's birthday was high on Kilol's agenda. After much forethought, she arrived at the conclusion that what her mother deserved as a birthday present was a pair of smart sandals. She decided to go with Lakhaan one day prior to mamma's birthday and purchase the above. 'There are 250 rupees in my piggy bank,' she sighed as she finished counting coins with the help of Laakhan. 'I'll take some money from papa,' she pronounced. Kilol goaded her father into parting with 500 rupees and gambolled her way to the market place with Laakhan alongside her.

'Be careful when crossing the road dear,' mamma spelt out as the two kissed each other good bye.

Kilol and Lakhaan entered a showroom displaying trendy and fashionable foot wear. After casting a glance at each one, Kilol eventually set her mind on a pink belle with a bow.

'How much does this cost?' enquired Kilol.

'Your choice is excellent! It costs 1100 rupees,' informed the storekeeper.

'But...but...I have just 750 rupees with me. Is there no discount available?' asked Kilol.

'Sorry....but the last offer price is 999 rupees. Take it or leave it,' declared the storekeeper. 'Why don't you take home a pair of amazing sneakers? If the person to whom you are gifting is a health-freak then these pair of lavender sneakers are just the right choice for her. Besides, an apron comes along with it free of cost and all of this at a ridiculous price of 700 rupees!!' said the storekeeper.

Kilol and Laakhan pleaded the storekeeper to wrap the sneakers and apron in an attractive packaging and Kilol delighted herself with an ice-cream worth 50 rupees on her way back home!

On Namrata's birthday, post the cake-cutting, the birthday girl unwrapped the gift that Kilol had brought for her and thanked her for being thoughtful and caring. 'Go and cram the table of 8 after you have finished eating the cake and don't forget to keep away the dishes in the sink after snacking,' Namrata instructed Kilol as she scurried into the kitchen to complete the heavy backlog of work.

After 20 minutes:

'All the while you are either playing with Rukmi, the maid's daughter or are absorbed in the virtual world. I have told you time and again to rinse your mouth well after snacking and you haven't cleared the plates from the dining area yet... Weren't you supposed to cram the essay I made you write 6 days ago... and...and...why is your play area is such a mess?' Then seeing Kilol tip-toe out into the portico with Rukmi while trying to avoid her mother's gaze 'Don't play with the stray animals as they are highly contagious.... finish your homework first and have your glass of milk before leaving....Killlooool.'

VENERATION AND THE PRICE OF AVARICE

Lokjeet Tyagi was a wealthy and opulent businessman who had amassed fortunes through sheer hard work, grit and determination. He and his wife were devout worshippers and had a shrine constructed within their campus precincts which boasted of idols of various gods and goddesses cast is semi-precious and precious metals. Rising at 5.00 a.m. in the morning and paying obeisance to the deities by way of chanting hymns, dedicating *bhajans* and meditating was their customary ritual for extending thanks for the Lord's bountiful blessings. Hariya, an old and trusted servant of the Tyagis, and Mrs Tyagi were entrusted with the task of cleaning up the shrine and keeping it in whiter than white condition. The box room next to Lokjeet's bedroom contained a chest which had lucre and precious jewels worth lakhs of rupees. Mrs Tyagi kept the keys of the chest in safe custody to which no one except herself, Mr Tyagi and Hariya could have access. Hariya alone had been made in charge of cleaning up the box room. Atop the treasure chest were statues of ancestral gods to whom Mrs Tyagi offered prayers daily to keep them in good humour.

Hariya's honesty and sincerity was unquestioning but of late he had acquired certain bad habits unbeknown to the Tyagis. He would keep late-nights playing card and drinking with likeminded individuals and the idea of misappropriating items from the treasure chest often bobbed-up in his mind to pave way for a lavish lifestyle.

One evening, while the Tyagis were partying in their garden downstairs, Hariya decided to give his plans the final shape. He served the hosts and guests drinks laced with sedatives, broke into Lokjeet Tyagi's box room and embezzled cash and ornaments worth *lakhs* of rupees. He had decided to collect his family from the village and abscond across the border to Nepal and never return. After he had finished executing the theft, he grabbed his bag and tiptoed through the hallway and stairway into the campus. He climbed the imposing walls, swishing away tiny beasts and venomous creatures amidst the thickets, and crawled down the fortification onto the lush-green meadows by the wayside.

At that time of the night, the roads were practically deserted and so it became easier for Hariya to creep away and hide his catch at a safe place where no one could discover it. Luckily, there was a graveyard near Hariya's house and he buried his catch there and retired to his room for some snooze. He spent the entire night tossing and turning. At 4.00 a.m. in the morning, he packed his luggage, had a quick bath and rushed to the graveyard to collect his bag. He dug beneath the Banyan tree but could find nothing there. In mad frenzy he dug here, there and everywhere but could not find the valuables.

'Did someone see me hide the bag and took it away in my absence?' he thought nervously.

Sun light filtering through the canopy forewarned him of the impending peril of being discovered and made him retrace his steps from the graveyard. He headed straight to the railway station and caught the first daily mail to his village.

Even in his village, Hariya could not sleep peacefully and was preoccupied with the thought that he would be caught and handed over to the police by the Tyagis. 'If the Tyagis come here looking for me, I shall narrate to them the entire tale and save my skin of the rigorous punishment that would otherwise befall me. Hope they are ready to believe my word...' he thought as he lay quietly on his *charpai* underneath the sky.

On the day following the theft, there was an uproar at the Tyagi's residence. Hariya's absence from the scene had explained it all. Mr Tyagi, accompanied by police personnel, left for

Hariya's village the same evening. When they reached there, they witnessed a large crowd gather outside Hariya's cottage.

'Where is Hariya?' inquired the police constable.

'Unfortunately today morning, while returning from the fields, Hariya was hit by a four-wheeler. He has been admitted to the city's government hospital and is in coma,' informed a villager.

Meanwhile, Hariya's wife stepped out of the crowd and muttered 'Sir my husband has not divulged much but I don't think he has your possessions. From the moment he returned from the city he seemed very quiet and tense...' and broke down.

'As you sow, so you reap,' said the constable. As for Mr Tyagi, he was lost for words.

The next day Mr Lokjeet Tyagi reached the city before dawn and after getting fresh, the Tyagi couple paid Hariya a visit at the government hospital. The visitors were allowed to see him only from a safe distance.

'He looks so pale and weak,' remarked Mrs. Tyagi. Mr. Tyagi stood transfixed, gazing at Hariya without batting an eyelid. The couple assured Hariya's son that everything would fall in place and left. For some days the incidence of theft was shut out.

A month later, a slow-witted boy named Dhanua expressed his wish to meet Mrs Tyagi. He had been an occasional visitor at the Tyagi's residence and would run errands for the family as and when required. That day, Dhanua was in a great mood and spoke to Mrs Tyagi at lengths on trifling matters. While Dhanua was around, he did most of the talking while Mrs Tyagi played the mute listener. 'Madam I witnessed Hariya scurry out of the graveyard with bag and baggage from the day that he went missing,' Dhanua whispered in Mrs. Tyagi's ear.

'Pardon me?' enquired Mrs Tyagi excitedly as she heard Dhanua dropping hints about Hariya's whereabouts from the day that he went missing.

Dhanua repeated 'I witnessed Hariya scurry out of the graveyard near his house from the day that he went missing. God knows what he had gone to do there?'

'Could this mean that the case of the stolen items was close to getting solved?' Mrs Tyagi thought. She instructed Dhanua to bathe the cows in the shed as it was a hot day and without a seconds delay informed her husband about the clue to the missing link in the valuables' theft case.

'From what I can gather, it appears that the bag of stolen valuables are not with Hariya. Then it is quite likely that he buried it in the graveyard and failed to recover it,' the police inspector opined.

'Then why wait. We must rush to the graveyard to find out the truth!' Mr Tyagi pleaded.

Upon reaching the scene, the inspector instructed his staff to dig-up the ground wherever they had a sneaking feeling.

The staff went in different directions.

After a few minutes Moin, a quick-witted sub-constable witnessed an 'H' marking on the ground behind Shamim's (a wealthy ivory merchant's) grave. He informed Mr. Tyagi and others about it. Mr. Tyagi at once informed Mrs Tyagi about the latest developments and thanked Moin for bringing the smile back on his wife's face.

There was jubilation at the Tyagis residence with Mrs Tyagi preparing special *prasad* to be offered to the deities and to be distributed amongst relatives, friends and mendicants of the city.

The following morning the inspector explained the case to the Tyagis at the breakfast table -'Such high were the levels of anxiety and apprehension in Hariya after executing the theft that he forgot having marked out the coveted spot with his initial. This is quite often the case with first timers in crime.'

Everyone else seated at the table had a good laugh over the situation except for the Tyagi couple who gave each other a dry smile.

HULABALLOO

Nandika, while pursuing her MBA course, was picked during campus selection to work in a reputed Multinational company. The happiness of her family members knew no bounds as it was a very lucrative and rewarding career option.

Nandika joined office in June 2012 and due to high competence levels was able to leave an imprint on her senior's minds and scale the professional ladders almost effortlessly. Besides, she was courting a guy for nearly eight years and the two had been very serious about each other so-much-so that Nandika had categorically stated in front of her parents that she would marry no one but him. Her parents did not openly disapprove of the match. Nevertheless they had their reservations as the boy hailed from a very different socio-cultural background.

Nandika had scores of friends and ganged-up with different ones each time that she had to catch-up with the latest movie or try-out cuisine at a recently inaugurated restaurant. Despite this, she had been a frustrated lot. Her main complaint was that her unceasing work hours and routine desk-job were not creatively rewarding.

'I'd love to do what the latest *bollywood* heart-throb did in the block-buster *Ye Jawani Hai Deewani,* that globe-trotting kinda thing you see. On second thoughts I could be a designer, sculptor or a curator in a museum,' she would repeat several times in front of family and friends.

Her parents, like every Indian parent wanted her settled like her siblings though. According to them, Nandika's professional and monetary status were enviable. So one evening when the family had gathered in the living room for the usual family discussion, Mr. Singh broached the subject succinctly and effectively — 'When we admire and appreciate the colossal beauty of the *Taj Mahal,* we fail to recognise the hard labour put in by 1000s of masons who built it. Likewise, we see the fame, adulation and veneration that the artists and designers enjoy quite overlooking the painful and difficult life they went through. You've worked so hard to secure this job and now you want to quit but always remember that a bird in hand is worth two in a bush.'

Nandika, who was awfully bored with the lecture excused herself on the pretext that she needed some rest and retired to her bedroom. Seeing her leave, Mr Singh cried out 'In your free time you can sneak a look at the biographies of famous designers on the internet to know the ground realities.'

Nandika locked her room from inside and began updating her *facebook* status. After a while her over-concerned father enquired 'Have you searched the internet for information on your favourite designers yet?'

'Yes definitely and it is quite an eye-opener!' replied Nandika who by that time was purchasing bras at discounted prices from an online portal!

The next day Nandika got ready for office and was looking pretty as a bride-to-be. She was going out on a date with her boyfriend in the evening and appeared more excited than ever. Her enthusiasm continued unabated for the whole week and on Friday during breakfast time Mr Singh enquired if everything was okay.

'I'm planning job hopping as I deserve a better salary,' Nandika informed.

'Hmmm, not a bad idea,' Mr Singh opined. 'May be I can be of some help in this regard.'

During the weekend while Nandika searched the internet for better career options, Mr Singh drew up an impressive Curricula Vitae for her. During the next few days, Nandika feigned illness and stayed away from work in anticipation of an interview call from big business houses but in the absence of any positive response she resumed office after a four days hiatus from work essentially to evade yet another lecture on the nuances of life from her voluble father. However, that evening she could scarcely evade questions from friends about her plans of quitting her current job for a more creatively rewarding career option. All at once a devil's face popped up in her imagination hinting her to manage her answers well. She smiled and said 'I am still learning the ropes!'

KASHVI'S DILEMMA

Kashvi was an intelligent and multi-talented banker who was adept in various skills from carpentry to fixing wiring problems in her house as also baby-sitting children in her immediate neighbourhood. However, she had one dreaded fear – the fear of cooking. From her childhood days she had loathed cooking and other kitchen chores. The culinary art was invariably Kashvi's mother's and brother Ragho's department who could churn up scrumptious recipes to suit every occasion.

Kashvi's father had been looking for a suitable groom for her and Kashvi had categorically stated: 'the household I am married into ought to have an army of servants to manage the kitchen chores.' 'You will eventually get married to a pauper,' brother Ragho would tease.

The year culminated in Kashvi's hush-hush wedding to a business executive who was based in Lucknow. The wedding was a private affair attended by a few relatives and close friends from the groom's and the bride's side. Post wedding, Kashvi moved in a rented flat in the posh Gomti Nagar area of Lucknow.

In the new set-up, Kashvi and her husband Samar left for their respective work places in the morning and returned late in the evening. At home there was an *ayah* to do the mopping and cleaning and a cook who could barely do justice to the routine *dal, chapatti* and *sukhi sabzi*.

One evening, Samar returned from office and informed Kashvi 'My boss along with his wife is expected for dinner tomorrow. Now the ball is in your court!' The news gave butterflies in Kashvi's stomach. With the assistance of her domestic help, Kashvi experimented with a few recipes that she had downloaded from the internet right away. After obtaining feedback from her husband and neighbours, Kashvi realised that her cooking was a disaster and eventually ordered meals from the assorted menu of a famous restaurant for the evening soiree. The menu also comprised of the famous *galawati kababs* from the Dastarkhaan hotel.

In the evening the guests were welcomed with mock tails and snacks comprising of mini cocktail *samosas*, fish finger with tartar sauce and mini pizzas.

While the men chewed over work and office politics the ladies discussed T.V. serials and shopping.

'Ma'am your *saree* is looking very nice. Where did you purchase it from?' Kashvi enquired.

'Oh, my brother got it from Noida. I do all my shopping from Delhi and Noida. My *bhai* and *bhabhi* live there and *bhabhi* keeps sending *sarees* and other stuff from there,' informed Mrs Sarcar, the boss' wife.

'This sea-green colour looks very good on you and makes your skin glow with health,' Kashvi uttered the flattering words.

'Why don't you come for the kitty parties that we organise every fortnightly. You will get a wonderful opportunity to interact with people and widen your social circle. I'll ask the hosts to personally invite you for the next meeting. Make sure you turn-up,' Mrs Sarcar enjoined.

'I definitely will madam,' replied Kashvi.

As the guests sat to have dinner, Mr Sarcar was all praises of Kashvi's culinary skills especially so of the delectable *galawati kababs* which melt almost effortlessly on putting in the mouth.

Assuring Samar of aggrandisement within due course, the guests took leave.

Kashvi's first appearance at the kitty party proved fruitful with new names being added to her list of friends. She was grateful to Mrs Sarcar for her concern and warm gesture.

As the *Teej* festival was drawing close, a special celebration had been organised by the members of the ladies' club to mark the occasion. The special feature of the event was the *Teej Queen Contest,* the dress code being green ethnic wear with the performance of *solah shringaar* held mandatory.

On the day of the event, the ladies arrived at the venue decked in *sarees* in beautiful shades of green as also traditional jewellery. They crooned folk songs, relished sweets and played a host of games after which it was time of the *Teej Queen Contest.* As the ladies came one after another demonstrating their talents, some provided invaluable cooking tips while others demonstrated how with some alacrity household wastes could be put to better use. This gave Kashvi the jitters. She didn't have the wildest idea as to how she would manage her act. During her turn however, Kashvi managed to regain her composure and explained how the various policies and schemes of her bank could benefit homemakers and wives of the current generation. This left the ladies seated in the room nonplussed and confused at first. However, Kashvi's articulateness and convincing style of explaining the various schemes of her bank managed to create awareness amongst women as to how with tact they could multiply their earning and increase their savings. The crowd burst into a wide round of applause after Kashvi's presentation with her being adjudged the winner of the beauty contest.

After the function, Mrs Sarcar requested Kashvi to be dropped at her residence as her driver was off duty that afternoon. Kashvi wanted to make a clean breast of everything but before she could start off Mrs. Sarcar interrupted: 'Those *galawati kababs* that we relished in your house that day were from Dastarkhaan...ha ha...we've been through all this at one stage in life but I am glad that you've been honest. Don't tell those ladies in the club about your weaknesses however or else they will make a mountain out of a mole hill! I'd suggest you joined the *Nutan Khurana's* Cookery and bakery classes. Those ladies in the club had also learnt cooking from there.'

'Is it madam?' Kashvi enquired with a look of wonderment.

'Then what did you think, they acquired the talent from their mother's wombs? Kashvi you really are so innocent.'

THE SILVER LINING

Megan had been upset over many issues of late – her mediocre grades, her failed relationships and the obstructive attitude of the people around her. The immediate factor that had triggered depressive thoughts and left her cornered though was her recent break-up with her long time boyfriend Frank.

Overpowered by edginess and suicidal thoughts, she could have chosen the easier route and ended it all. However, her die-hard optimism to keep going in the face of adverse circumstances was exemplary. She approached the college counsellor Mr Sam Menon for the much needed moral support.

'You seem to be in a pretty doleful mood Megan; what is the matter?' enquired Mr. Menon.

'A string of unpleasant events have opened the can of worms in my life and have rendered me feeling hapless,' informed Megan.

'Explain everything?' pleaded Mr Menon.

Megan wept as she narrated her ordeal and explained as to how she was trying hard to deal with the situation all by herself with no help at hand.

Mr Menon who was both experienced and a shrewd judge of people peered through his thick-rimmed spectacles fallen over the bridge of his nose and laughed aloud 'Your problem is insignificant and your worries overstated.'

Offering her a glass of water, he gave her a list of assorted activities to choose from. The stimulating activities helped melt away Megan's angst. She found strong positive vibes emanating from Mr Menon and his spiritedness hugely infectious!

It took just a few counselling sessions to revive Megan and bring her back on her two feet perkier than ever.

After clearing her class twelve exams, Megan wanted to study no more. She applied for a receptionist's job and got the call letter within three days of putting-up the request. However, she became tired of wearing a plastic smile and entertaining tedious questions put forth by visitors day in and day out and eventually quit her job from a few days of joining.

Luckily, from the advertisements on hoardings and posters, Megan learnt that the time for the reality show *'Zara Nach Ke Dikha'* season 8 was drawing close. With the encouragement of friends and Mr Menon, Megan realised that it was time to put on her dancing shoes! As far as dancing was concerned, Megan had abundance of chutzpah and was a celebrity in her own right.

'Who will be my dancing partner?' she tried to think hard and realised no one other than Frank her ex, fitted the bill. Their sizzling chemistry was talked about within the nook and crannies of the college corridors.

'Shall Frank agree to become my dancing partner? Megan asked her friends. 'If only we could come together for the show and set the stage on fire, it would be wonderful!'

Megan's friends promised to influence Frank into becoming her dancing partner for the reality show and returned with positive news in a short while. Megan's happiness knew no bounds.

During the reality show, Megan and Frank were rated highly on all departments but one. 'The poor on-screen chemistry between the two of you is one of the reasons why you may miss out the coveted trophy,' the judges of the reality show chorused time and again.

At that time the dancing couple realised that emerging victorious in the show required more than just extraordinary dancing talent and they needed to spend more time in each other's company to rekindle their waning chemistry.

Hard labour yielded results and on the day of the grand finale, their lissom and supple bodies melt in one another's arms like two artistic-gymnast virtuoso performing. This resulted in Megan winning not just the coveted trophy but also the hearts of millions of fans and more importantly Frank's.

After their victory, Megan and Frank were thronged by the paparazzi from all sides and the couple were tired of answering the endless cross-questioning by the media persons.

When posed with the million-dollar question as to how she would utilize the prize money she had earned post winning the show, Megan gave the pert reply

'I will start a dance academy for children where young girls and boys from poor families will be imparted training in the field free of cost. There is no dearth of talent in our country but numerous children are denied access to the vocation of their choice due to lack of funds. Now they need not worry on that count!.' Megan's initiative was lauded within the corridors of homes, offices and educational institutions.

Megan was definitely amongst a few of the chosen ones.

OVER THE HORIZON

CHAPTER 1

Her audacity in handling the grim situation of turning away the covetous groom from the marriage altar in a quintessential filmy style had made her a heroine overnight. The media persons had thronged her house to capture the melodramatic scene in their cameras and to record her message to be displayed as an example for the fairer sex to follow. The putting up of a brave act had had mixed reactions in the society though. The orthodoxy had condemned her behaviour and had dismissed it as unreasonable and such as those defying societal norms. There were empty speculations regarding her marriage prospects seeing the end of the road.

Her kin had stood by her as pillars of support hoping that there would be light at the end of the tunnel.

Walking down the college corridors and the market place had become irksome due to constant gazes and indiscriminate murmurs. Piya was pursuing her graduation with Sociology honours and had of late entered the final year of her course. However, the new developments had left her very distracted and she was unable to put her mind to studies. Very recently, her friend Kajal was planning to get enrolled at a prestigious college in Mumbai and had requested Piya to join her. Piya had begun considering the option seriously as what she needed was a breath of fresh air during those trying times. Her father's permission was all that she needed to set the ball rolling.

Stealing time from Mr. Kushal Sharma's busy schedule was a tricky affair and Piya would have to wait till Sunday to put forth her request. Sunday was three days away and in the meantime Piya had been thinking of the best possible manner in which to broach the subject. She sought her mother's and brother's support in handling the exigency.

On day three, when the entire family was seated at the dining table for lunch, Piya decided to intervene: 'Daddy I wish to enrol in a college in Mumbai...Kajal is also keen... maybe we can do it together. Moreover, you are quite aware of the situation here. This is academically a crucial year for me and I'm unable to put my mind to studies...'

Kushal did not exhibit any outward reactions and refrained from commenting on the situation. He quickly gulped whatever was in his plate and retired to the lounger for an afternoon siesta leaving others nonplussed and confused.

Kushal continued to maintain silence on the subject during the evening at tea-time as also at night during dinner time. However, the next day before departing for work he eventually broke his silence: 'We all realise that our family, more so Piya is going through troubled times. I had a heart-to heart talk with your mother last night and we both agree that our children have made us proud with their achievements whether academic or otherwise. I can consider the option of sending you away on the condition that you will hold on to the family values and not let the indecorousness of city life tarnish your pristine mind.'

Piya made a promise that she would assimilate only the best that the city life had to offer and steer clear of all that was vulgar and unbefitting a girl from a respectable family background.

With this preparations for going to Mumbai began in full-swing. Mother and Piya went to the most fashionable stores in Patna to purchase clothes and accessories that they thought would be in sync with the pulse of the city. Her brother Aditya instructed her to be in touch via phone calls and *smss*.

The day when she had to kiss goodbye to her family members finally arrived. Her mother Astha hurried with the basket of fried *pooris, aloo sabzi* and Piya's favourite lime pickle for the train journey. Her elder brother Aditya helped her with the last minute packing and Kushal carefully steered his Maruti Alto out of the garage whose seating capacity was five average built persons. Astha took the seat next to Kushal's while Piya, Aditya and Kajal occupied the rear ones. Thanks to their lean and mean physiques, they were all easily accommodated.

Thankfully, the road connecting the Sharma's home to the railway station was smooth and non-rickety, an otherwise uncommon sight in Patna.

Having arrived at the railway station, the girls collected their luggage and scurried towards the platform where the train had halted to accommodate boarding passengers. Piya bade farewell to her parents and sibling with drenched eyes. As the train chugged along the tracks, Piya's kin found it hard to hold back their tears. Piya and Kajal ate their tiffins and shared a light banter before retiring to their berths for a power nap.

CHAPTER 2

The train reached Mumbai within a day and a quarter. Piya and Kajal felt very elated to be in a city which was home to many a *bollywood* stars. They appeared starry-eyed about the manifold opportunities that the city had to offer. The tall sky-scrapers and the wide roads took them by surprise, the incessant rains had somewhat marred the fun though. In the evening, when the rains had abated they went for a ferry-ride from the *Gateway of India*, fed a flock of gurgling pigeons and tried having coffee at the Taj, but the exorbitant prices made them look for cheaper options and they eventually settled for a quaint restaurant at *Colaba Causeway*. The girls ambled down the promenade at Marine Drive and even witnessed the Queen's Necklace known for its splendour since the bygone days. The next day it rained heavily and the weatherman warned the *Mumbaikaars* to stay away from the sea. This thwarted the girls' plans to go for yet another splash!

Piya and Kajal were putting up at the latter's aunt's place till they had sought admission in a reputed college and had found an appropriate hostel accommodation. The admission season was over in the Mumbai colleges. The girls were on the lookout for somebody well-connected who could see them through. On a Tuesday morning in mid July, they paid obeisance at the *Siddhi Vinayak Temple* and by evening their prayers were answered. Kajal's cousin's friend Deepak who knew the college Principal well played the guardian angel and helped them get hold of management quota seats through the use of sheer tact, diplomacy and excellent communication skills. The girls thanked Deepak fervently. Very shortly Piya and Kajal were able to find a reasonable hostel accommodation for themselves.

As Piya and Kajal were pursuing different streams, they got paltry time to spend with each other during college hours. Kajal, the more accommodative of the two, made friends easily. However, Piya was in for a cultural shock to witness scantily clad young ladies fagging in public. If the unbearable stench of smoke had sent her coughing to the doorstep of the Pulmonary Physician's clinic, the condescending manner and the double standards of the rich babes of her college were not any less putting-off!

Among many, she chose the gregarious Rishika and the down-to-earth Manya to be her friends. The two girls were very different from the rest of the crowd and were very helpful and supportive towards college freshers.

The head-to-toe *salwar* clad Piya earned a *behenji* image within the college corridors. Her introversion was a protective shell which helped her stay away from all that was vulgar and brassy. Only her close friends knew of her bold and intrepid side and realised that she could bring the city's traffic to a halt with her rain dance!

CHAPTER 3

It was rose day in college and it was quite a spectacle to witness fashionably dressed young ladies receive roses from dapper gentlemen. It was equally amusing to witness the young crowd throng the florist's shop and bicker with the florist over the prices of roses.

'Every year there is a shortage of roses at the florist's shop. In the morning, the prices of the flowers sky-rocket and by evening they plummet as the demand for the coveted flower falls,' informed Manya as she exchanged roses with Piya.

After spending a few hours in the library pouring over books, Manya and Piya sneaked into one corner of the campus to witness the activities of the day. The large rose bunches in maiden's hands and an equal number strewn on the floor gave passers-by the impression as though there was some flower festival going on!

Piya who was looking fetching in a pastel pink *kurti* and blue *chudidar* and *dupatta* received a great many roses that day which made her realise that she was more popular in college than she had imagined. Among the gentlemen who offered her roses was the lean and swarthy Mayank and the cute and adorable Rustam. While Mayank was the winner of the previous year's college personality contest, Rustam's USP was his Parsi descent which made girls hover around him like bees around flowers. Ironically, Manya sporting the T-shirt which said '**I'm fat because you don't deserve me**' received amusing glances and the least number of roses that day!

College life offered a slew of entertaining events and opportunities for young adults to showcase their talents. These were the inter-youth college fests, college socials and the enchanting *dandiya raas* celebrations among many.

'Sieze every opportunity that comes your way,' father and friend Rishika advised.

Piya had begun to realise that life in a metro wasn't some sort of a cake walk and she would have to walk that extra step to make her life more exciting and eventful.

'I'm here to stay. I like Mumbai despite its foibles. Returning to Patna is not an option worth considering even in the wildest of dreams!' she thought as she reflected upon the wonderful piece of advice offered by family and friends.

'I'll explore the *dandiya raas* this time,' Piya said as she jumped out of bed one autumn morning. *Dandiya Raas* which had its roots in the traditional Gujarati folklore had enticed Piya ever since her school days. Interestingly, the suave Mayank (who had offered Piya flowers on Rose Day) had offered to be her dancing partner.

'Mayank is a Gujarati and you will have to infuse perfection in your dance moves to match steps with him,' said one of Piya's classmates.

'If this is a challenge I am ready to face it headlong and prove my detractors wrong,' she said as she clashed sticks with Rishika in the ladies common room.

After an hour of practice Rishika commented 'Although you have grasped the steps well, the synchronization part will have to be worked on. Come-on, let's treat ourselves with some cold coffee and *wada-pav* in the canteen after the back breaking work!'

Within a matter of few days Rishika had transformed Piya into a dancing diva. On the day of the *dandiya raas* event, Piya had teamed a red mirror-worked backless, yes **backless** *choli* with a yellow *lehenga* with black motifs and a green *dupatta*. That evening her dance and clothing style made quite a few heads turn and gaze in wonderment as to how the *behenji* of yesterday had metamorphosed into a lady with the oomph factor!

To everyone's surprise, Piya and Mayank also won the best dancing couple award that evening. The two however were by no means destined to be real life couples as the ever-so practical and down-to-earth Mayank made her realise that he was only one of Piya's admirers and not to be taken seriously. Her brief courtship with Rustam did not last more than a couple of weeks on account of Rustam's popularity with the opposite sex which made his girlfriends very insecure and self-effacing. Piya had the maturity to take all her failed relationships in her stride and was enjoying her 'single' status. Thankfully, the men in her life were mature and respectful enough as not to give her an emotional baggage.

CHAPTER 4

Post merriment and festivity it was time for hard labour as graduation final-year exams were drawing close. Pupils were witnessed discussing work in the nook-and-cranny of the college corridors. Piya was a dedicated and sincere student and a favourite with the professors. They had hopes that Piya would put the college's name in the Hall of Fame with her astounding performance. Post exams, Piya went to Patna after a lengthy hiatus to spend time with her loved ones. Back home she was welcomed with the lingering aroma of home-cooked food, something she had been missing all along in Mumbai. Granny presented her a hand-embroidered blouse almost stitched to perfection. When teamed with a pair of figure-hugging denims, it gave her an air of confidence and she blurted out the lines that reflected her own wishes and aspirations 'Rishika feels I am cut out for modelling.'

'Your ideas are quite far-fetched. Thank heavens that your father is not here or else he would bring you to book. He wants you to choose an academic line,' Astha muttered as she whisked curd to prepare *chaas* for granny and Piya.

'Take a chill pill *maa*. Standing at five feet eight inches and with those credentials, daddy will have a difficult time finding a suitable groom for me here!' quipped Piya.

Incidentally, that evening Kushal was very emotional and like a typical *Bihari* parent divulged his secret wish to Piya: 'Your brother went against our wishes and joined the Air Force. We sincerely hope that *you* will do us proud by qualifying in the Civil Service Exams. It was your grandfather's wish that one of you joined the IAS.'

At night Piya gazed at the stars from her bedroom window thinking as to whether she had the inner strength to sacrifice her wishes and longings for the general interests of the family. She was searching for the answers within when her granny lying beside her realised her predicament and shared side-splitting stories to brighten and cheer her mood. 'People in our society cannot think beyond Engineering, Medicine and the Civil services as viable career

options,' granny chuckled. The two spent the entire night gazing at the stars and discussing topics that they had not done in a long time. In granny's presence, wistful memories of childhood days when her wishes were fulfilled at the drop of a hat by her doting uncles and her unceasing appetite for fables was satiated by her grandpa and grandma, became reminiscent in Piya's mind's eye.

Vacations were over even before Piya knew it. She cleared her graduation final-year exams with flying colours and had the realisation that the time for chasing butterflies in the garden was long over and that she would have to get her act together and reach for the skies. She returned to Mumbai and shifted in a two-bedroom apartment with Rishika. Rishika helped her grab modelling assignments with a reasonable pay-packet. However this was not enough given the myriad challenges in a bustling city and Piya was always hard-pressed for money.

Moreover, after learning about her current professional status, Piya's father had stopped sending her pocket money. Her mother Astha would sometimes send her some money from her savings but that was not enough. Unfortunately, this time Piya's friends Kajal, Rishika and Manya had to be content with *sambhar-wada* and appy fizz on Piya's 22nd birthday which by no means was a grand celebration like all previous years. Piya had made a promise to her friends about returning the following year with a larger-than-life birthday bash to make-up for the current year's low-key affair.

The current misfortune did not deter Piya in the least from chasing her dreams. On the contrary she was resolved to leave her foot print in her chosen field of activity. With a few modelling assignments in her kitty, she had ample time to pursue her passion 'painting'. She led a recluse life honing her skills as a painter and chose socially sensitive topics as subjects for her artwork. Her artworks reflected the sufferings, aspirations and hopes of the common man of modern India. Juggling of roles between modelling and painting had drained her physically but that was what a struggler's life in a metropolis all about.

Patience and hard labour yielded rich dividends when her talents were recognised and ended her sufferings both financial and psychological. Her paintings were well-received by admirers and critics alike. This made her parent's chest swell with pride and express apology for committing the sin of misconstruing her intentions.

Piya spent a portion of her hard-earned income in purchasing goodies for family members as her deep-rooted Indian values had taught her to put family before all else. She deposited a large portion of her income in her savings account and spent the remainder on shopping and partying with a handful of friends in a city which in quite a few ways was her own yet in so many ways a total stranger.

CHAPTER 5

Piya took exit from her rented accommodation and shifted into her newly purchased flat in Andheri-east with roomy interiors and fresh sunshine and breeze. However, the most important people viz. her father, mother and brother were missing from her house-warming party guest list. The reason was her brother Aditya's secret marriage to a war-widow two months ago which had rendered her hypertensive father upset and disturbed. Her father was not as much perturbed by his choice as he was with him having kept the marriage a secret and eventually getting the news from third parties. Ever since the disclosure of the news, Aditya had refrained from calling his parents let alone visit them. He had not contacted Piya either and the latter had been anxiously awaiting his call to explain the situation on the home front.

If Aditya's bizarre attitude was worrisome, then equally vexing were the troublesome mice and the occasional rats which had made Piya's apartment their playing field! Kajal who would drop-in at Piya's residence off-and-on to spend time with her howled at the maid 'Leela, why did you not purchase a mouse trap with the money that Piya gave you yesterday? Need we repeat the same thing over and over again? Did your husband happen to beat you yet again last night after getting drunk...?'

However there was no noise from the kitchen except the clattering of utensils. Within minutes Leela entered the living room flashing her thousand-dollar smile and two bowls of mouth-watering *kheer* for the ladies. 'Madam, I have finished the day's work. Today morning, there was a cultural programme in my daughter's school and I was busy helping her with the rehearsals yesterday and today. If I fail to purchase the mouse trap by tomorrow you can punish me the way you wish? I'll definitely do the needful; it is a promise.' Leela said as she plodded out of Piya's apartment shutting the door behind her.

'Getting a good maid is a luxury these days. Leela *bai* is honest and good-hearted but can be a bit lazy and careless at times,' Piya opined.

I swear by her cooking, the *kheer* that she has prepared is toothsome! My best wishes to strong women like Leela who have the patience to tolerate their foul-mouthed and nagging spouses. I would not tolerate such a man even for a split second,' remarked Kajal.

'Sweet people are often the most mistreated,' remarked Piya.

After a few seconds of quietude marked by the gentle blowing of breeze and the occasional frisking of mice, Kajal intervened 'There is a small get-together party at my friend Neil's house. I got introduced to him through a common friend. He hails from a business family and takes keen interest in photography and painting. I have spoken to him a lot about you and he has asked me to bring you along tomorrow.'

'I'm not a party animal sort of person. You can go ahead and enjoy the day,' Piya said as she got hold of a novel by Margeret Mitchell and straightened her sofa-cum bed for some relaxation.

'You are going to miss something if you do not attend. Once you get there, you are going to love it...I swear,' convinced Kajal.

'I shall give it a thought and let you know by tomorrow,' Piya said as she switched-off the main lights and turned on the table lamp to enjoy the book before her. The mice gambolling about and playing made her attention wander somewhat. She smiled and said 'Aren't they too cute and puny?"

Kajal refrained from commenting and lay in bed pulling the sheet of cloth over her body to ward-off the cool breeze. At that point of time all she could fancy was the Pied Piper play his mystical tune to ward-off the meddlesome mice menace!

The next evening, the ladies chose their outfits carefully to befit the occasion. While Kajal chose to go all in black, Piya teamed a midnight blue layered top with biege cigarette pants and matching accessories. Kajal's hair was done in a twisted coil while Piya had done it into a French knot and the wispy bangs falling over her face accentuated the softness of her immaculate visage.

The ladies were welcomed at Neil's Bungalow with fresh fragrant flowers and tamarind-flavoured mock tails. The leafy precincts, the verdant landscape and the musical fountain left them beguiled. This was followed by a performance by a famous *sufi* artist as the guests relished savoury snacks. Before the dinner was laid, the guests were invited on the dance floor to sizzle and sway to foot-tapping numbers. From amongst the bevy of gorgeous ladies, Neil danced with Piya the most.

'I am very passionate about bird watching and photography. From what I can recollect you... arrre...a professional painter.' Neil remarked.

'Yesss....' Piya looked away as her attention wandered to the description Kajal had provided about Neil 'Why did Neil not mention about his paintings...or was this one of Kajal's ploys to get me to the party? Doesn't matter, I shall have ample time to get even with her once we get home,' Piya thought pursing her lips and crinkling her forehead into a frown.

Neil, in an attempt to revive Piya said 'Come along to witness the displays of my modest artworks that I have created so far.'

Piya followed in Neil's footsteps and the two requested Kajal to join in. However Kajal, who by now was aware of the sizzling chemistry between the couple did not want to become an undue interference and asked them to carry on.

Upon entering the hallway, Piya was awestruck by the lofty ceilings and the arched hallways that bespoke of the architectural marvel of the British bygone era.

'My great grandfather purchased this house from the British way back in 1939.'

The labyrinthine pathway led to a stairway at the end of which was a room boasting of Neil's imposing displays.

On the walls were depicted photographs of the various species of migratory birds such as the painted storks, the black headed ibises, the cormorants, herons, flamingos and the spotted pelicans as also the garden birds such as the parakeet, the tailorbird, the oriental magpie robin, the drongo, the purple sunbird and last but not the least the house sparrow whose falling numbers in many parts of the world is noteworthy.

Piya wanted to wade through the wealth of information about each one and witness the sparrow shelters which Neil had put up in his courtyard but had to leave at the Neil's mother's behest to join them for dinner right away.

Piya took small servings of food-items in her plate from the assorted buffet spread laid out and occupied one of the round tables to enjoy her dinner and the lilting music playing in the background. Although Piya could not have an eyeful of Neil's mother who showed-up only for a few minutes, she was floored by the hospitality of his sister Nina who was showing personal interest in each guest. After a while, Piya was disturbed by the indiscriminate murmurs at one of the adjoining tables.

'Her clothes are mismatched and she dances so awfully!' remarked one of the ladies while others in the group sniggered.

On giving an earful, Piya realized that it was she that the ladies had been criticising. She gave her clothes, hair-do and make-up a cursory glance in the hand mirror that she was carrying in her clutch-bag. While on her way home, Piya was almost reduced to tears and regained her composure with Kajal's assurance that there was nothing wrong with her dress sense or dancing and the ladies who had been criticising her were only jealous of the attention she was getting from the rich and fine-looking Neil and needed to redefine their sense of style.

CHAPTER 6

Back home Piya had been too peeved with the ladies at the function for their bitchiness to pick a fight with Kajal for lying about Neil's hobbies. However, the good news was that Neil had been showering on her too much love and attention these days. Sighting the lovebirds at the movie theatres, parks and restaurants was becoming a usual occurrence. Even when they did not get time to meet each other due to their time-packed schedule, they were constantly in touch on *facebook* and via *sms* texts and telephonic conversations. If Neil was trying to get to know Piya in a better fashion, Piya's homogeneous interests extended to encompass Neil's immediate family members as well. She was extremely beguiled by the polite and affable Nina and gentle-looking Mrs Raj Shekhar, Neil's mother.

God had been very generous in granting Piya's wishes these days as Nina arrived at her doorstep to get her portrait made no sooner than Piya had asked for it. This entailed Nina taking several rounds of Piya's house at the end of which a strong rapport was developed between the two ladies. Nina was all praises of Piya's talent which resulted in a bee-line of prospective clients at the latter's doorstep to get their portraits made. This proved a boon in Piya's career and was monetarily very rewarding. Piya could figure out that Nina was scarcely aware of the relationship status she enjoyed with Neil and regarded them as just great buddies!

One evening, while taking Neil's dog Rover for a stroll, the lovebirds reached the leafy outskirts of the city and the heavy downpour forced them to seek shelter in a hutment comprising of a tattered cot, an earthen pot half-filled with water, smelly clothes fastened onto a peg and a bundle of sticks piled up in one obscure corner. Having quenched their thirst, the lovebirds lit a small bonfire to ward-off the shivers brought about by their partially drenched clothes, an aftermath of the freakish weather.

As Piya wiped her hair with her stole, her long tresses cascading down her cheeks gave her a classic and ethereal appeal which was quite irresistible to Neil.

'D...do you have something to eat, I'm extremely hungry?' enquired Neil.

'There are some eatables lying in my handbag. You can take a look at it,' Piya answered flashing her perfect set of white teeth.

Neil could witness that Piya's handbag carrying multiple pockets which among many comprised of food items, a kerchief, multi-tool kit, a personal organiser, a makeup kit, few keepsakes and old bills of the window and online shopping she had done some while ago. 'A woman's handbag is an amazing store-house for things both relevant and inconsequential!' Neil thought as he drew out an apple from the bag and cut it into thin slices to be shared among Piya, Rover and himself.

'Rover does not like apples,' Piya quipped as she threw a handful of dog biscuits before him and while the dog relished his favourite meal, Neil realised that good-looking people like Piya often ran the risk of being overlooked for their compassion and fellow feeling.

The storm proved to be a blessing in disguise as it brought two souls even closer and two hearts skip a beat as one.

From her ambivalent attitude towards the Mumbai city during the initial months of arrival, to falling head-over-heels in love with the Mumbai-born elitist Neil Raj Shekhar, Piya had indeed come a long way.

'Love comes as a surprise package when we least expect it and we all become helpless at the hands of fate,' Piya thought.

After the storm had abated, a gaunt looking watchman with a lantern in his hand entered the hutment.

'These leafy precincts belong to a church. Please do not forget to pay obeisance at the church before leaving for home. It's me Robert D Costa, the guard,' said the watchman.

'Thank you so much for the tasty water that we sipped from the earthen pot and the safe shelter to shield us from the bad weather,' Neil greeted.

'It is all by God's grace. It his him you should thank,' said the watchman.

The couple attended the prayer meeting and the choir singing at the chapel and on their way back home, did not fail to appreciate the beauty of the church building, the well laid-out garden the lush-green meadows and the thickets of forest cover washed clean by the pitter patter.

However, on reaching Neil's home, Piya and Rover had bouts of sneezing and coughing spells and Piya had no option but to spend the night at Neil's bungalow. Neil administered over-the-counter drugs for Piya's niggling symptoms. Piya, Neil and Nina went for a rock concert late in the evening where the artist crooned *Turnover* and the *Blueprint* by *Fugazi* band, *Just like you imagined* from the *Nine inch Nails* album, *Invisible* by *U2* and a few of his compositions amidst the strumming of guitars and the beating of drums. Nina by now was able to figure out the sizzling chemistry brewing between Neil and Piya from their verbal and non-verbal cues.

CHAPTER 7

Neil who was the owner of men's clothing stores and restaurant chains known by the name 'Cinnamon Sticks' across Maharashtra had been facing flak of late due to spurious content of the food and drinks served in his restaurants. Relatives of victims who had been hospitalised after consuming adulterated food and drinks had approached the Consumer Court for speedy justice. Neil who had been in the above business for nearly a decade and had enjoyed an unsullied reputation had engaged his most trusted servants to look into the matter and identify the culprits expeditiously. As a result of the above incident, Neil had incurred huge losses and was at sixes and sevens. On close examination it was discovered that a lot of confidential data had been tampered with. His most trusted men were suspecting his cousin and arch rival Sudhanshu Ranjan's hand in the offence, however he could not be brought to book for want of evidence.

In the worst-case scenario a certain section of Neil's so-called "well-wishers" had begun to regard Piya as a star-crossed ally. Neil had been trying hard to retain his composure in the most trying times and planning a weekend getaway to Goa to celebrate Valentine's day as proposed by Piya didn't seem such a bad idea to him.

Before heading to Goa in Neil's private jet, Piya was taken by surprise to receive a call from her brother Aditya after a long hiatus.

'Adi where are you?' enquired Piya in a concerned voice.

'I'm serving as a flying officer in the Indian Air Force and am off to Congo as a part of the United Nation's Peace Keeping Mission,' informed Aditya.

'What about your wife?' questioned Piya but Aditya's phone had blanked out and could not be reached despite several attempts. Disheartened, Piya left the message 'Get in touch with mamma immediately as daddy is not keeping well these days.'

In Goa the love birds were putting up in a private resort overlooking the sea. It was Carnival time in Goa but the pristine location of the resort was a tranquil paradise for lovers hitherto unheard of.

The lovebirds enjoyed the water sports such as parasailing, snorkelling and fishing and dined at the 'Laguna' restaurant in the afternoon and at the Seafood restaurant during the night. They played catch-and-throw in the resort's private pool, Piya looking smouldering in a teal bikini with pink polka dots and Neil showing-off his sinews in an ebony-black swimming trunk. Piya was happy to witness Neil's worries vanish away in thin air while still wondering whether her message had reached Aditya. She tried calling her brother and mother continually but they could not be reached due to poor connectivity.

On Valentine's eve, the couple decided to keep the celebration simple and sweet. The house keeping staff had decorated their cottage with balloons, streamers and fancy Chinese lights. An arrangement for candle light dinner had been made in the balcony and the aroma of sweet-smelling roses adorning the dinner table and the fresh breeze added to the romantic mood.

The couple danced arm-in-arm to groovy music while relishing sparkling beverages. At this time the eyes did most of the talking while the lips parted to meet zealously. During that minute Neil wished secretly that the opportune moment would go on forever and ever. After the lovebirds had been worn to a frazzle by too much dancing, they sat at the table and relished meals which were a blend of Italian and Continental fare prepared by Piya in the kitchenette provided for the purpose. Piya seemed doubtful of her culinary skills at first but felt poised with Neil's assurance that she had managed to put up a pretty decent act.

After the meals Piya wanted to dance more but Neil insisted on playing *Jenga Truth-or-Dare.* After creating the tower, Piya picked a red block which said 'Say the alphabet backwards.' Piya to Neil's surprise gave out her lines like the *Rajdhani Express* in full momentum after which it was Neil's turn. He carefully pulled-out a green block and read 'The most daring thing you've ever done.' Neil held Piya's hand and confessed 'I love you Piya from the bottom of my heart and I think uttering these words is the most awfully daring thing I have ever done.' Piya turned crimson as she pulled out another red block. She read aloud 'swap an item of clothing with someone'. Piya refused to oblige while Neil went on to insist that she played in accordance with the rules of the game. Following this a pillow fight ensued which lasted a good ten minutes and ended with the mellifluous chirping of birds atop trees in the resort's sprawling campus.

'It's day break,' Piya said as she hurried to the rest room to become fresh while Neil enjoyed watching the sun rise over the horizon cast a fuzzy reflection over the azure sea. Very shortly Piya joined in and the lovebirds captured the historic moment in their cameras. After getting ready for the day, the lovebirds unwrapped the Valentine's gift that they had hidden behind the cushions to surprise each other.

Neil's gift to Piya was a diamond encrusted ring and the print version of her personal memoirs.

'How did you find out all this? How did you manage to sneak into my bedroom and get hold of my personal diary?' Piya hollered with a look of astonishment on her face. 'Thanks anyway, thank you so much,' she said flashing her endearing smile.

Neil returned the look of surprise to receive his portrait where he was depicted in a business suit looking pensive and thoughtful.

On Valentine's day, the couple enjoyed taking a walk on the sun kissed beaches with the occasional sighting of gulls preying on tiny fish and shrimps swimming beneath the sea surface. At noon time they went for a relaxing massage at the spa and late in the evening they purchased goodies from a souvenir shop to be distributed among family and friends.

Back in Mumbai, Piya found a string of *sms* texts from her mother lying in her messaging folder the excerpts of which were:

'Aditya had called at your behest. He is leaving for Congo in a few days time. His wife has entered the third trimester of pregnancy and is presently staying with her brother's family in Amritsar. I shall be leaving for Amritsar in the coming month as your father seems to be recuperating from his illness at a steady pace.'

Piya heaved a sigh of relief at the favourable turn of events.

CHAPTER 8

After their adventuresome trip to Goa, the frequency of meetings and *sms* texts had diminished between the lovebirds as Neil had been too busy resolving his business issues. Neil's indifferent behaviour had not perturbed Piya in the least only till he had closed all channels of communication with her let alone answering her phone calls and *sms* texts.

'No matter what the circumstances or the situation, Neil would always find time for me. Is it so that he has started believing in the 'unlucky' tag thrust upon me by certain others,' Piya who was intelligent enough to realise what the rumour mongers had been spreading behind her back, thought for a split second. The loving words uttered by Neil time and again reverberated and echoed in her dreams and left her unsettled.

Overpowered by negative emotions and unable to bear the brunt any longer, Piya rushed to her friends for some solace. Piya's friends Kajal and Rishika were always there for her during her difficult times trying hard to assuage her pain with comforting words:

'I've known Neil from the past one year and from the little knowledge I have of him I think he is not a guy given to gossips and rumours. He probably would be too involved with work to think of anything else. Even I haven't had the opportunity to speak to him for days,' remarked Kajal in Neil's defence.

'Men are more practical than women in love and enjoy the chase when women are more unpredictable. Some men dislike women who are clingy and emotional types and the best way to get them is to keep them guessing. I'd suggest you let go-off for some days and see if he comes back,' quipped Rishika.

'And what if Neil does not return,' enquired Kajal.

'All we can do is wait and watch for the water to settle under the bridge,' suggested Rishika.

'I have a feeling that Neil is mature enough to realise what's best for him and will eventually
realise Piya's importance in his life,' Kajal reassured.

Assuring Piya that things would turn out in her favour, her friends departed.

Piya's friends managed to dispel her fears only partially. Nevertheless, Piya decided to give Neil his space. In the meanwhile she painted on the theme 'fear' which was an outward manifestation of her supposed phobia of losing Neil. The painting made headlines and was sold for a whopping 3 crores to an industrialist who was an art aficionado.

Piya also volunteered in to be a part of the cleanliness and tree plantation drive an initiative taken by social activists of her city. She was roped in to design the logo for the 'Clean and Green India' campaign. Various movie stars and models wielded brooms against dirt and disease and showed their green thumb by planting thousands of trees. Piya could relate the happening with Neil's penchant for birds as trees, a pollution and dirt-free environment and our feathered friends are invariably interconnected. This brought tears in her eyes.

CHAPTER 9

The next morning it was flashed in the newspapers that Neil's restaurant fiasco was on the verge of being cracked. The prime accused Sudhanshu Ranjan and his allies had been held and were being interrogated by the police.

In the meanwhile Piya's friends were always by her side and maintained that she was not perturbed any further by the separation anxiety from Neil. After a few days Piya bumped into Neil at the supermarket where he had turned-up with his mother for the monthly grocery shopping needs. He pursued Piya relentlessly, avoiding glances from his mother, trying to explain the reasons for his extended absence from the scene. However, Piya pretended to be in a hurry and dismissed all his clarifications as lame excuses. Grabbing her arms he drew her in one corner and gave her an honest and intent gaze that pierced her soul and provided answers to questions she had yearned so long. With some effort she managed to escape from his clutches though and while letting go Neil could feel the diamond ring he had presented to her still aglitter on her finger, demonstrating her boundless love for him.

Back home Piya was surprised at the unanticipated arrival of Nina and Kajal at her doorstep during evening time.

'Neil's absence from your life for a few days, or a few months for that matter does not imply that he has walked out of your life. He is always there for you even when he seems very very far. This is what true love is all about and he wants you to understand that,' explained Nina with a down cast look.

'I guess you were being over-anxious and reading too much into his behaviour. By avoiding him, you are running away from the truth and depriving yourself of the beautiful moments which life has offered at your doorstep,' said Kajal. 'You are scarcely aware of what Neil has been through all these days. Aunty's (Neil's mother's) best friend Suman was keen on having Neil as her son-in-law. Neil wanted to say no to this proposal but at the same time did not want to hurt

his mother. He had decided that he would make a clean breast of his current relationship status to Suman aunty's daughter Rati when a meeting was arranged between the two. Thankfully however, during the meeting, Rati divulged that she had finished her graduate programme in Bioengineering from the Harvard School, was keen on doing research in the above field and did not want to get married and settle down right away. Rati asked Neil to reject the proposal as Suman aunty was not ready to understand her daughter's point of view...so... Neil turned down the proposal with the lame excuse that he could not marry a girl who liked capsicums as he hated the vegetable and could not tolerate it in his meal every day and night. He also said that he was on the look-out for a girl who was more homely type!'

Piya, Nina and Kajal had a good laugh over this one.

'Neil is leaving the country tomorrow to negotiate an important business deal so if you feel his need in your life, please get in touch with him today as he may not be available for you in the next few months', informed Nina and ambled out of Piya's apartment with Kajal following close at her heels.

After her friends had left, Piya reflected upon their words and realised that Neil was a mature youth who deserved every bit of her affection and decided to make the necessary amends before it was too late. Piya picked-up the phone to call Neil when the instrument buzzed flashing her mother Astha's number on the screen.

'Aditya has just arrived with his wife Ratna and your new born nephew at our doorstep. You must congratulate them both,' Astha said handing over the phone to Aditya.

'Congratulations on the arrival of a new member in the family. I am planning to join you in Patna in the next few days,' informed Piya.

'Thanks, thanks a lot,' Aditya grinned as he handed the phone to Ratna.

'Many many congratulations. I can't wait to see you and my nephew. I'm coming to Patna in the next few days,' informed Piya.

'Yes please do as the baby's initiation ceremony shall be half-baked without his *bua's* blessings,' Ratna insisted as she disconnected the phone.

Piya called Neil who informed her about his mother's discovery of their affair from the proximity they had shared at the supermarket and her willingness to meet Piya at the latter's residence for tea the next evening. The lovebirds congratulated each other for being in an enduring and long standing relationship and Neil dismissed rumours of his foreign trip as work of Nina's and Kajal's imagination to get their act together!

The next morning, Piya set out with the preparations for the evening affair without further ado and with Kajal's and Nina's helping hand, she had little to worry about.

GLOSSARY

1. *paratha* — (in Indian cookery) a flat thick piece of unleavened bread fried on a griddle.
2. *bahurani* — daughter-in-law
3. *bollywood* — the Mumbai film industry
4. *pulao* — a Middle eastern or Indian dish of rice cooked in stock with spices, typically having added meat or vegetables
5. *pari* - fairy
6. *bindi* — a decorative mark worn in the middle of the forehead by Indian women, especially Hindus
7. *namaste* — a traditional Indian greeting or gesture of respect
8. *memsaab* — a title for a woman in position of authority and/or wife of a *sahib* (a polite title or form of address for a man)
9. *kaka* — uncle
10. *amma* — a way of addressing an elderly woman; also means 'mother'
11. *bhajans* — devotional songs
12. *charpai* — cot
13. *prasad* — a devotional offering made to God, typically consisting of food that is later shared among devotees
14. *ye jawani hai deewani* — a famous Hindi movie
15. *dal* — in Indian cookery (split pulses), in particular lentils
16. *chapatti* — (in Indian cookery) a thin pancake of unleavened wholemeal bread cooked on a griddle
17. *sukhi subzi* — a vegetable without gravy

18. *galawati kebab* – a dish from South Asia made of minced goat meat and green papaya, traditionally used to tenderise meat. It is the hallmark of *Lucknowi (Awadhi)* cooking.
19. *samosa* – a fried or baked pastry with savoury filling, such as spiced potatoes, onions, peas etc.
20. *sari* – a garment consisting of a length of cloth elaborately draped around the body, traditionally worn by women from South Asia.
21. *bhai* – brother
22. *bhabhi* – sister-in-law
23. *Teej* – a festival celebrated in Northern India during the monsoon season when women observe fast for husbands, adorn themselves and sing songs
24. *solah shringaar* – the 16 adornments of an Indian Hindu bride, which contribute to her complete beautification
25. *puris* – (in Indian cookery) small round pieces of bread made of unleavened wheat flour, deep-fried and served with meat and vegetable
26. *aloo subzi* – vegetable cooked with potatoes
27. *Mumbaikaar* – the inhabitants of the Mumbai city
28. *Siddhi Vinayak Temple* – A famous lord Ganesha temple situated in Mumbai
29. *salwar* – a pair of light, loose, pleated trousers, usually tapering to a tight fit around the ankle worn by women from South Asia worn with *kameez/kurti*
30. *behenji* – is a respectful term for sister. Also used in a derogatory sense to denote unfashionable, uncool and housewifery sort
31. *kurti* – a piece of loose shirt falling either just above or somewhere below the knees worn by women of South Asia

32. *chudidaar* – tight trousers worn by people from South Asia, typically with a kameez or kurti

33. *dupatta* – a length of material worn arranged in two folds over the chest and thrown back around the shoulders, typically with a salwar kameez, by women from South Asia

34. *dandiya raas* – a type of traditional Gujarati dance in which pairs of dancers hold a short stick in each hand and strike one another's sticks in time to music

35. *choli* – a short sleeved bodice worn under sari or with lehenga by Indian women

36. *lehenga* – a full ankle-length skirt worn by Indian women, usually on festive or ceremonial occasion

37. *chaas* – a buttermilk preparation from India

38. *maa* – mother

39. *Bihari* – people hailing from the state of Bihar in India

40. *sambhar wada* – a savoury South-Indian dish

41. *kheer* – a South Asian rice pudding made by boiling rice, or vermicelli with milk and sugar.

42. *bai* – maid

43. *sufi music* – the devotional music of the Sufis, inspired by the works of Sufi poets like Rumi, Hafiz, Bulleh Shah, Amir Khusrou and Khwaja Ghulam Farid

44. *Rajdhani Express* – a series of fast passenger train services in India operated by the Indian Railways connecting New Delhi with other important destinations

45. *bua* - paternal aunt